MW01614532

WINDY

by

Patricia Henry Crutchfield

FIRST EDITION

UNIVERSITY EDITIONS, INC.
1905 Madison Avenue
Huntington, West Virginia 25704

Cover and interior art by Joan Waites

Dedication

I would like to dedicate this story to my Grandpa, Floyd Leach, who is now watching over me from heaven. Thank you for planting the seed. And to my two wonderful daughters, Charity and Kellie, who allowed me to enjoy childhood even more the second time around.

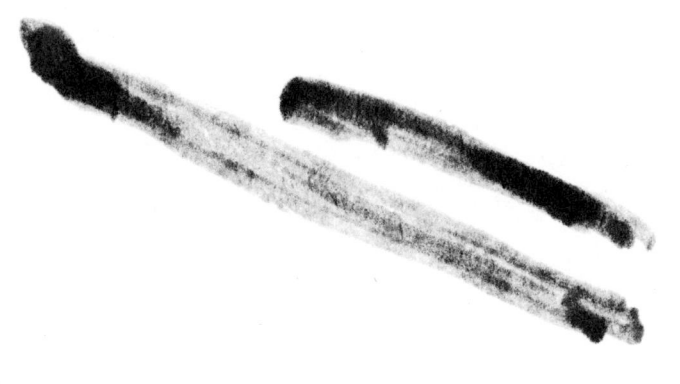

Did you ever lie in the soft green grass, on a warm summer day, watching the clouds blow softly by? Do you remember how your imagination seemed to run wild as it pictured elephants, lions, and whales floating majestically through the sky? Have you ever wondered why some of the clouds seemed to be trimmed with a heavenly light? When I was a little girl I thought those clouds were big soft cotton like pillows the angels would rest on after a hard day at play. The light that seemed to trim them was really the radiant light from the angels, shining through.

Have you ever wondered what a cloud could be thinking as it floats through the sky, looking down at you?

Windy was a small, light, fluffy cloud born above the foothills of the Appalachian Mountains. She felt lucky to have been born in such a beautiful place.

Windy enjoyed seeing the fields that dotted the countryside; a patch of alfalfa here, a field of corn there, some wheat or hay over there. To Windy it looked like one great big patch work quilt. The red barns added just the right accent.

One day when Windy was out playing with the trees, gently blowing her soft breeze through their branches, she noticed some children playing over by the creek. Some of the children were using stepping stones to cross the creek. They were pretending it was a river full of alligators, and if they should slip off of a stone, they would surely be eaten. Others were stooped along the edge of the creek, catching pollywogs in a jar.

"What fun," Windy thought to herself. "I wish I could play with the children."

It was a warm sunny day. The children seemed to be enjoying the cool of the creek water. They didn't even notice Windy. How could she get their attention???

"Chil-l-l-ldren," . . . she whispered. A soft breeze blew gently from her mouth. "Chil-l-l-ldren," . . . . she whispered again.

The children seemed to hear her whispers. They stood up, running, laughing, and turning in the cool breeze.

"What fun," Windy thought. "I love the children most of all. I think they love me too."

Evening came. The children had to go in. Windy felt sad; but she knew the children would be back outside in the morning. Windy thought, "If I can

keep a mild breeze blowing, the children will stay cooler and sleep better. Then they will feel more like playing with me in the morning.

That night Windy's big brother Mike moved in . . . "Move on!" . . . Mike said as his much stronger winds blew Windy farther and farther from her beloved Appalachian Mountains. . . and the children she grew to love.

As day light approached, Windy's fears grew. She was in a place so different than she had ever known. The air was brown and heavy. It didn't have the sweet smells of clover and pines, like the mountain home she was used to. Instead of lovely red barns scattered across green fields, there were dirty gray buildings, clustered together. She noticed lines and lines of noisy machines. "Beep, beep, veroom, veroom," they said.

Windy was afraid. She was so afraid she didn't notice that she had grown into a large thunder head. Windy started to cry. She cried so hard, that people say she cried two inches of rain on the city that day.

Windy's big brother Mike was still behind her. . . . "Move on, . . . Move on," . . . he cried, as his bigger winds blew her on.

As Windy's tears dried up, she realized she was small again, just like when she was at home in the Appalachian Mountains. Oh, how she missed those mountains, and the children that lived there. She would probably never see her mountain home again.

"Hello Windy." said a pleasant voice. It was Aunt Kate. She had blown down from Canada. "Why do you look so sad?" Aunt Kate asked.

"I miss the lovely foothills of the Appalachian Mountains. I miss the children, and the Trees." said Windy.

Windy didn't realize Aunt Kate was a north wind. She was swiftly blowing Windy back to her mountain home.

"Look Windy!" said Aunt Kate. There are your children. You are home."

Windy was so happy. . . .

If you go to the foothills of the Appalachian Mountains today, you will see the children and hear their laughter, as the clouds gently blow a breeze through their hair.

46

If you look up in the sky I am sure you will see
Windy, softly calling, "Chil-l-l-ldren, Chil-l-l-ldren."

THE END